Seeing Green

Adapted by M. C. King

Based on the series created by Michael Poryes and Rich Correll & Barry O'Brien

Part One is based on the episode, "More Than A Zombie To Me," Written by Steven Peterman

Part Two is based on the episode, "People Who Use People," Written by Michael Poryes

Bath · New York · Singapore · Hong Kong · Cologne · Delhi · Melbourne

First published by Parragon in 2008
Parragon
Queen Street House
4 Queen Street
Bath BA1 1HE, UK

ISBN 978-1-4075-4649-0

Printed in UK

PART ONE

Chapter One

Miley loved her best friend, Lilly, but sometimes the girl could be indecisive – unbelievably indecisive.

They'd been standing at the mirrors in the girls' toilets for practically all of their free period while Lilly played with her hair, unable to find a style that worked. Miley felt for Lilly, she *really* did. Everyone has had a bad hair day, after all. Still, Miley could think of so many better ways to spend their time – not to mention, more pleasant places to spend it in. Sheesh, she thought. When was the last time they cleaned this place?

"Behind the ears . . . over the ears . . ." Lilly waffled while puzzling over her reflection. "I know . . . one behind, one over."

Miley couldn't take it anymore. She was haired-out. Plus, she had news – huge news! She needed to get Lilly's attention. "*Uuhhghh* . . ." she moaned, making a crazy face into the mirror.

Lilly was still in her all-about-my-hair mode. "Hey, it's not that bad," she said defensively.

"*Uuhhghh!*" Miley got even louder.

"Okay, all right," Lilly said, untucking her hair from behind her ears. "No ears."

Lilly was one of the smartest girls Miley knew, but she could be surprisingly dense sometimes. "Lilly!" Miley exclaimed. "This

isn't about your ears. I'm trying to tell you something."

"What?" Lilly cracked, examining Miley's pained expression. "Your trousers are too tight?"

Only Miley's nearest and dearest knew her secret: that she was *more* than just your average middle school student; that, outside of school, she had a whole other identity and life as Hannah Montana, one of the biggest teen pop stars on the planet. Miley checked to make sure the coast was clear, then lowered her voice just in case. "Guess which famous pop star is going to play Zaronda, Princess of the Undead, on *Zombie High*?"

Lilly had a tendency to be sarcastic. "Paula Abdul?" she ribbed. She and Miley both watched a lot of reality TV, so she knew Miley would get the reference to

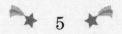

their favourite judge on *American Idol*.

Miley double-checked underneath the cubicles. She didn't see any feet. "No, Hannah Montana!" she answered.

"That is so cool!" Lilly exclaimed, looking truly excited for a second. Then Miley's news finally hit her. "But, wait, you don't know how to act," she blurted out.

"What are you talking about?" Miley asked. Did she really have to remind Lilly about how much she acted? "I act every day. I act like I'm not Hannah Montana. I act like Oliver's jokes are funny." And then, because she couldn't resist, she added: "Yesterday, I acted like I liked that sweater you wore."

"What?" Lilly looked stricken.

"Just kidding," Miley teased. "I loved it! See? I was acting." She looked slyly at Lilly. She couldn't help messing with her head. "Or, was I?"

Lilly got the point. "Ooh, you are good," she said. "Hey, do you have any scenes with Jake Ryan?"

Not counting Miley – and you couldn't count Miley, since most people didn't know she was Hannah Montana – Jake was the school's biggest celebrity. He acted in movies and just so happened to be the star of the popular TV show *Zombie High*.

Jake was supercute in a perfect-looking, blond, surfer-boy kind of way. Miley had to admit she was a sucker for a beach boy – except Jake was also totally and completely full of himself. As Hannah Montana, Miley had met a lot of head-swollen celebrities and Jake was just about the worst, she thought.

Just thinking about him made her mad. "I don't know," she said, answering Lilly's question about whether she had any scenes

with him. "I haven't got the script yet, but I don't care. I get enough of that egomaniac at school."

Lilly wasn't buying it. "Oh, come on. You so like Jake."

"I do not," Miley protested. "How can you say that?"

"Because every time his name comes up, you 'act' like you can't stand him."

"That ain't acting," Miley assured her.

"Or is it?" Lilly teased.

"No!" Miley insisted.

Lilly shrugged. "Then you're the only girl at school who doesn't have a crush on him."

"Oh, please," Miley scoffed. "I think people are starting to see through his phony little game."

As sick as Miley was of having this conversation, she was more sick of hanging out

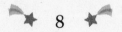

in the toilets. She straightened out Lilly's hair, then dabbed a little lip gloss on Lilly's lips, and ushered her best friend out of the door.

Lilly hadn't been joking about every girl at school having a crush on Jake. When they left, the first thing they saw was him surrounded by a group of girls. "Ladies, please, no crowding," he said, puffing out his chest. "Sally, Wendy, Yolanda, you know the rules, before noon only names that start with A to L."

Miley watched in amazed horror as a dejected Sally, Wendy and Yolanda shuffled off. Sheesh! Who did this guy think he was?

The only other student at Seaview Middle School who knew Miley's secret was her other best friend, Oliver Oken.

 9

Oliver bounded over to them. "Hey, have you guys heard?" he asked excitedly, gesturing towards Jake and his fans. "Sometime today Jake's gonna ask one lucky girl to the Seventies Dance. As soon as he picks one, there'll be a hundred depressed girls lookin' for a shoulder to cry on." Oliver grinned while patting his own shoulder. "Here it is, broad and water-absorbent."

Miley and Lilly rolled their eyes at once. There was one thing they could say about Oliver: when he saw an opportunity, he took it.

"Look at him," Miley said with a sneer, motioning to Jake. "It's disgusting."

Lilly still wasn't buying it. "Oh, come on, if he asks you to the dance, are you telling me you wouldn't say 'yes'?"

"Yes," replied Miley with a definitive nod.

"Yes, you'd say 'no'? Or, yes, you'd say 'yes'?"

Arrgh! Lilly was making her head hurt. Now she couldn't remember the question. Oh, yeah, if Jake asked her to the dance, would she really say no. Miley thought for a second. "No!" she said. *Ack!* That's not what she meant! "Yes, I'd say 'no'!"

Right?

Miley didn't have time to think anymore about this, because moments later, someone, a guy, *was* actually saying: "Hey, Miley, you wanna go to the Seventies Dance with me?" Huh? It took Miley several seconds to realize it wasn't Lilly posing a hypothetical question. It was Jake Ryan, the actual Jake Ryan, who'd asked. He was standing before her; his posse of girls had followed him over. Mouths gaping, they awaited her answer.

Did she want to go to the dance with Jake Ryan? Miley's brain thought, "No way." But for some reason her mouth said, "yes."

The girls groaned.

Miley got a hold of herself. "I mean no," she said.

The girls cheered.

Jake looked dumbfounded. It was as if he'd never heard the word before. "No?" he asked in disbelief.

"Yes," answered Miley clearly. "I mean no."

All the girls looked at each other, confused. No? No! Could it be she actually meant to say no to Jake Ryan? *The* Jake Ryan. Miley turned to the girls. What were they waiting for? "Now you cheer," she instructed. They happily complied.

And then, to show Jake just how much

she really meant it, Miley grabbed Lilly by the elbow and walked off.

"No?" Lilly asked, when they were out of earshot.

"Yes," replied Miley.

"Yes?" echoed Lilly.

This was getting beyond annoying! "No!" Miley said. "Now stop that!"

At this point, her head was pounding.

Chapter Two

When Miley got home, the *Zombie High* script was sitting on the kitchen table. Her first real script! Miley hadn't even taken it out of the manila envelope before rushing off to Rico's to show Lilly.

Rico's was the most popular place to hang out on the beach. Still, it was never *this* crowded. What was going on? As Miley got closer, she realized she should have known: Jake Ryan was what was going on. Miley's "reject" was relaxing under the outdoor shower, wearing board shorts and a rash guard. Meanwhile, groups of girls gawked from every available vantage point.

Miley thought it was funny that Jake was acting oblivious to all the attention. As someone who was often in the public eye, she knew he could feel all those eyes boring into him. She also knew he positively loved it. Not only did Jake thrive on attention, he clearly lived for it.

Miley found Lilly, staring at Jake as well, looking positively entranced. "Lilly," she whispered. "Guess what I got?"

Lilly shushed her. "Not now. Jake's about to change."

Oh, no, Lilly had the Jake bug, too! "Into what?" Miley challenged. "A decent human being?"

"No, he's gonna take off his rash guard,"

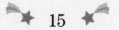

Lilly responded breathlessly, without looking away.

"But Lilly, I just got the script for *Zombie High*!"

This news got Lilly's attention. "No way," she said, grabbing for the envelope. "Let me see it."

The girls surrounding Jake let out a gasp. "Oh, man," Lilly groaned, looking up to see that during the one second she'd looked away, Jake had changed from his rash guard to a hoodie. "I missed his muscles!" she cried. "His zombie-slaying muscles!"

Miley shook her head. She couldn't believe Lilly had succumbed. "Lilly, build a bridge and get over it," she said, trying to sound harsh but not *too* harsh.

Lilly's eyes found themselves back on the script. "Oh, my gosh, look at the title of the episode, 'Forbidden Love.' I wonder if that's you!"

Miley hadn't even considered that possibility. "It better not be," she said, feeling more than a little apprehensive.

A shadow loomed from above. Hey, who took the sun away? Miley wondered. She looked up and got her answer: Jake Ryan, of course.

"Hey. What's up?" he said.

Miley had the script for *Zombie High* in her lap. Yikes! She quickly slipped it under Lilly's butt. "Nothing, just a magazine," she said, covering.

"What?" he asked.

"Nothing," she snapped. "Hi."

"Listen, about the dance," Jake said. "You seemed really nervous when I asked you, which is to be expected, 'cause, you know, look at me." He grinned.

"I do . . . all the time . . ." Lilly gushed. "Even when you don't know I am. . . ." She looked confused. Turning to Miley, she asked, "Did I say that out loud?"

"Yes," Miley said sternly. What was Lilly's problem? The last thing Jake needed was *another* girl fawning over him.

"I just wanted to give you a second chance," Jake said, as if he were doing her a giant favour. "So, you wanna go with me?"

Someone needed to take this boy down! "Jake, I wasn't nervous then." Miley talked very slowly in the hope that he might actually absorb the information. "I'm not nervous now. I just don't want to go to the dance with you."

"So that's a 'no'?" Jake still looked confused.

"Yes."

"Yes?" Jake asked with a smirk.

"No." Miley tried not to giggle. "Now stop that."

"Okay. But I want you to know, I'm shooting an episode with Hannah Montana this week. And even though I'll be kissing her, I'll be thinking of you."

And off he went.

Sometimes Miley could be a little dense herself.

"Can you believe that guy?" she huffed. "Trying to make me jealous by saying he's gonna be kissing Hannah Montana. . . ." She stewed in momentary indignation, then realized what she'd just said. "Wait a minute." There was panic in her voice as she grabbed the script back. She rifled through it until she got to the page she was looking for.

"Oh, no!" She gasped.

"Oh, yes!" Lilly cheered. She was reading over Miley's shoulder.

"This is horrible," Miley said. "Not only do I have to kiss him, but my lips fall off."

Lilly kept reading. "No, it's okay," she said when she got to the bottom of the page. "See," she pointed to the director's note. "He reattaches them with his love."

"*Ewwww!*" cried Miley.

"*Awwwww*," cooed Lilly.

Chapter Three

Mr Stewart chuckled as he returned the tape and scissors to the kitchen drawer. Usually he got his daughter, Miley, to wrap gifts. Who knew it could be so satisfying? In fact, he was so enthralled with his handiwork, he didn't hear his son, Jackson, come home.

"Hey, Dad. What you got there?" Jackson asked, pointing to the package with the perfect bow that was sitting on the worktop.

"A birthday present for Uncle Earl," he answered.

"Oooh, cool, can I see?" Jackson asked, going for the box.

Mr Stewart lunged forward to try to stop him. "Son, don't open that, don't open that –"

Too late. When Jackson removed the lid, the box emitted a giant sucking sound – like an industrial-strength vacuum. Mr Stewart looked in horror as his son's head disappeared into the box. "Turn it off, turn it off!" came Jackson's muffled cries.

Mr Stewart checked his watch and counted: "Three, two, one . . ."

The vacuum stopped. Jackson removed his head and stared, shocked and red-faced, at his dad. "What is wrong with you?"

Mr Stewart tried not to laugh. "I'm sorry, son. I told you not to open it. You know how Uncle Earl always sends me a prank for my birthday. Well, this year I decided it was time for a vacuum-packed payback."

Someone else might not have been so quick to forgive. But Jackson was always up for a good time. "Oooh, can I get in on it?" he asked.

Mr Stewart chuckled. He loved that his son enjoyed a joke as much as he did. Still, he was just a kid. "Jackson, no offence, but this game's for the big boys. Uncle Earl is one of the all-time great pranksters. I think you should stay out of it. I wouldn't want you to get hurt."

Jackson looked shocked. "You're saying you don't think I have what it takes to put one over on Uncle Earl?"

It appeared his firstborn needed a reality check. "Son," said Mr Stewart, "you couldn't even put one over on your old man."

Jackson took a moment to let his father's words sink in. But if he felt their sting, he didn't show it. He simply smiled and shrugged. "Gee, Dad, I guess you're right," he said, bidding a hasty retreat. "Well, see you later!" he called.

Uh-oh, Mr Stewart thought when he noticed a telltale gleam in Jackson's eyes. He called after his son. "Jackson, I know that look!" he warned.

"What look?" Jackson asked innocently. "Bye!" he shouted, leaving his father alone with his vacuum masterpiece.

Mr Stewart smirked. "Something tells me this ain't gonna be pretty," he mumbled to himself. "But it might be fun."

Chapter Four

Five hours in make-up! Miley had to admit sitting still for so long while a make-up artist layered her cheeks with foundation and powder had helped her get into character. Her face felt frozen underneath all the gunk; her jaw hung slightly open from the weight of the latex they'd attached to her lower lip. She hadn't even rehearsed and she already felt like a zombie.

Boy, making a television show required a

lot of waiting! Miley was sitting in a director's chair next to the make-up table, watching actors shoot a scene she wasn't in, when the director came over to introduce himself. "Hi, Hannah, I'm Roger, your director, big fan, big fan. You look horrible. It's fantastic!"

Miley was a pro, and she knew the last thing you were supposed to do, upon meeting the person in charge, was to complain. But she'd thought about this a lot and felt she had to say something. "Listen," she said in her politest voice, "I've been thinking about the script and I've just got one little problem –"

"Oh, boy . . ." Roger sighed. She was pretty sure she saw him roll his eyes, too.

Miley wasn't trying to be difficult; she really wasn't. "No, it's just a little thing," she said. "Do I really have to kiss that zombie slayer?"

Miley was expecting a one-word answer, but what she got was an elaborate and geeky sci-fi explanation. "Well," said Roger, looking very serious, "since the divine prophecy states that only by reawakening the cold, dead heart of the princess can the slayer rout the forces of darkness and save the world from ultimate destruction, I'm going to have to say yes, you do."

"But why does he always have to save the world?" Miley asked. "I mean can't his faithful sidekick, Demon Dog, save it this week? I would rather plant one on the pooch."

"Interesting idea," Roger told her, though Miley could tell he didn't mean it. "I'll mention it to the writers. But for now, just try to have fun. And remember, all of us here … big fans, big fans."

She watched as Roger crossed the room

and moved towards Jake. She couldn't hear everything they said – though she managed to make out a couple of phrases here and there, like "diva guest star" and "nervous about the kiss" and "put on the charm."

Well, that backfired, Miley thought, watching Jake as he strutted towards her, no doubt to "put on the charm." She readied herself for the cheesefest.

"Hi, Hannah, I'm Jake Ryan," he said, reaching out to shake her hand. "We're so thrilled to have you on the show this week."

"Yeah," said Miley, worried for a second that Jake might recognize her voice. Then she remembered it was Jake Ryan; the guy barely listened to anyone. "It's gonna be really interesting for me, too."

"So what do you think of the script?" Jake asked.

This guy was so fake! "Well, I love everything except page forty-one," Miley answered. She was being blunt – she didn't care.

"Oh," said Jake with a nod, "the kiss."

"Yeah, nothing personal, buddy, but –"

Jake interrupted her. "Man, this is not my week," he said with a sombre shake of the head. "I mean, first, this girl I like won't go to the school dance with me, and now my zombie princess won't kiss me."

"Yeah, well, I just don't think The Zombie Princess . . ." Miley was so stunned she interrupted herself. "Who's this girl at school?"

"Her name's Miley," Jake answered.

Miley was glad she was wearing pounds of white make-up. Otherwise, he'd have seen her blushing. "Wow. What an interesting name. I've never heard anything like it. She must be really unique." It was funny: she often had to talk about Hannah Montana as if she didn't know her, but she had never had to talk about Miley as if she were a stranger. It felt completely alien and totally weird.

"She is," Jake said. "She's cute and funny and smart – she's so down-to-earth. When I talk to her, I feel like she's not talking to Jake Ryan the celebrity; she's talking to Jake Ryan the guy. You know what I mean?"

Actually, Miley knew exactly what he meant! That was one of the reasons she didn't let anyone know she was Hannah. Everyone was always kissing up to Hannah Montana and she was never sure whom she could trust. It was annoying.

Even more annoying was that Miley couldn't talk about this with many people, because complaining about people sucking up to you was downright obnoxious. But Jake seemed to understand. She felt her defences melting a little bit. "Yeah, I do," she murmured. "Sometimes you need to know people like you for who you are and not just because you're a star."

Jake looked shocked. It was like somebody was finally getting it, getting him. "Exactly!" he exclaimed. "And she doesn't like me as a star or as a person. Isn't that great?"

Wait, wasn't this the guy who thrived on everybody worshipping him? "Uh . . . is this a trick question?" Miley asked.

"No, it's just, it's something new to me. Look, I'm really sorry I'm dumping all this on you, it's just, I can't stop thinking about her."

"Really?" She was reeling.

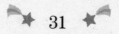

Jake shrugged. Then, sounding unusually defeated, he said, "Well, I guess I'm just gonna have to forget about it."

Because she didn't know what else to do, Miley agreed. "Uh, yeah, right, I suppose forgetting about her is good."

Jake got back to business. "So, back to this kiss. Just close your eyes and count to sixty. It'll be over before you know it."

"Sixty?!" Miley shrieked.

Two seconds later, Roger called "Places!" and Jake was spritzing breath spray into his mouth. "Hope you like thunder mint," he said.

Sixty? That was a really long time.

Back at the Stewart house, Mr Stewart was making a habit of talking to himself. He stood over the table, lifted the domed lid off the cake plate and eyed the half-eaten layer cake. Dressed in a track-suit and trainers, he was about to go for a jog, but he needed a little incentive.

"Darling," he told the cake, "in three and a half miles, you're all mine." He took a lick of icing, then rethought his proposition. "Maybe just three. What the heck, maybe I'll just jog down to the end of the drive-way, get the mail and be right back." He placed the lid back on the cake plate and set off for his jog.

Moments later, Mr Stewart returned with the mail in his hand and his prize in clear view. "Come to Papa," he told the cake.

Except this time, when he removed the lid, there was no cake on the plate. Instead there was Jackson's head in the centre of a doily. His mouth was smeared with choco-late icing.

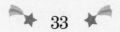

As Mr Stewart gasped in horror, Jackson let out a triumphant "Booyah!"

It took Mr Stewart a couple of seconds to get his bearings back. He looked at his son laughing devilishly and thought about how the kid had no idea, no idea at all.... Now he was messing with the big boys. "Your life is about to get real interesting, son," he said.

Jackson stood up. Having sawed a head-sized hole through the table, he was now having a hard time getting out. So he took the tabletop around his neck with him as he went to the refrigerator to get a glass of milk.

He needed to wash down all that cake.

Chapter Five

It was only Take One and things were going pretty well. Miley wasn't used to memorizing lines and she was pleased to see that all her hard work had paid off. She'd got through her scenes with the evil ghouls, who were just about to shove her into the portal that delivered her to the underground. Now the Zombie Slayer, aka Jake Ryan, came crashing through the door to save her. "Dudes!" he cried. Miley had to admit he sounded pretty convincing. "I slayed you once. Looks like I'm gonna have to slay you again."

Wow, the guy even did his own stunts! She couldn't help admiring Jake's martial arts skills as he slayed the ghouls. "Zaronda!" he cried when he was finished. Miley was impressed – Jake hadn't even broken into a sweat! "Are you okay?" He reached down to untie her. She fell limply into his arms. Their faces were but inches apart. He held her close. His arms felt so big . . . and strong . . . and . . . finally, Miley realized it was time for her big line!

"For a dead girl I've never felt so alive," Miley said breathlessly.

"Then why did you run away from me?" Jake asked, staring deep into her eyes.

For a split second, Miley actually believed Jake Ryan was The Zombie Slayer. Who knew he was such a good actor? Maybe he was a lot smarter than he let on at school. Maybe there was a whole secret side to Jake.

Miley stared back into his eyes. She'd never seen such a beautiful shade of blue. "Don't you see? Our love is forbidden. We can never be together."

"Then maybe this will change your mind," Jake said as he moved his face even closer to hers.

Miley's body wasn't moving, but her brain was going at top speed. He really is cute, she thought. And he thinks I'm cute ... and down-to-earth. But then she recalled the Jake she knew offstage. The Jake that paraded around school like he was better than everyone else, who encouraged girls to traipse after him. She had to get a hold of herself! Oh, stop it, Miley. You don't like him, she thought. Then again, it was important to be honest with yourself. Oh, who am I kidding? Yes I do, she thought, reconsidering. And then his lips were nearly touching hers.

"Cut!" Roger called. "That's lunch!"

Miley looked around, her lips still pursed. "What? Wait, wait, wait!" she cried. "What about the kiss?"

Roger came on to the set. "I thought about it and you're right. We should see how the audience feels about the relationship first – then bring you back."

It was exactly what Miley had wanted. Keyword: *had*. "But –" she spluttered.

"In the meantime, after lunch, we'll try that kiss with Demon Dog." And here she'd thought Roger hadn't even listened to her. "Hope you don't mind the taste of kibble and gravy. He's a messy eater."

Jake caught up with her. "Wow, Hannah, you were great in that scene! You really looked like you wanted to kiss me." If he only knew, Miley thought. As she headed for lunch, all she wanted to eat was . . . her words.

Chapter Six

Miley was beyond happy to see Lilly. She'd called her about a zillion times both last night and this morning, but there had been no answer. It wasn't like her best friend to be so unavailable. And Miley had so much to tell her about her day on the set of *Zombie High* – not to mention her new-found feelings for Jake.

Finally, she'd found Lilly, wet from bodyboarding, on her way to grab a bite at Rico's. She bypassed "Hello" and got straight to the point. "Lilly, I've been calling you all morning! Why haven't you been answering your mobile phone?"

"My dad took it away after the last biology test," Lilly explained sorrowfully. "Who knew photosynthesis had nothing to do with photography?"

"Everyone," replied Miley. "Now do you want to hear about *Zombie High* or not?"

"Yes, yes, yes!" Lilly said eagerly. "Tell me everything! But start with the kiss! How was the kiss?"

"Wet and kibbly," answered Miley, who then explained the whole Demon Dog disaster. "But that's not what I wanted to tell you. It's about Jake. I realized that I actually –"

Miley desperately wanted to tell Lilly that she had been so right – Miley *did* like Jake! Lilly had accused her of it and it was about time Miley admitted the truth. Plus, she needed Lilly's advice, because now Miley was considering asking Jake to the dance.

As if her thoughts had conjured him up, Jake appeared before them. "Hey, guys," he said.

It's fate, Miley swooned, thinking she'd have to live without Lilly's advice just this once. It was time to seize the moment.

"Look, Jake, about that dance thing –" she started to say.

"Don't worry, Miley," Jake interrupted. "I'm not going to ask you again. I've learned my lesson."

Learned his lesson? Wait! What lesson? "Oh, really?" she balked. "Because I was thinking –"

He interrupted her again. "That I should

move on, I know. That's why I came over here to ask Lilly."

To ask Lilly?!

Miley watched in horror as Jake turned to face Lilly. Lilly beamed expectantly. "Do you wanna go to the Seventies Dance with me?" he asked.

It took Lilly less than a millisecond to answer. "Yes!" she practically yelled.

"Cool," Jake said happily. "I'll call you with the deets."

Miley stood still as Lilly fizzed with excitement. Did what she thought just happened really just happen?

"I'm going to the dance with Jake! I'm going to the dance with Jake!" Lilly squealed.

Miley knew she should be happy for her best friend, but she couldn't help feeling grim.

Lilly noticed Miley's sombre attitude. "Why aren't you happy dancing?" she asked.

Miley paused for a moment. She couldn't think of any other explanation. "Because I like Jake," she answered honestly.

Lilly stopped dancing. *"Since when?"* There was an edge to her voice that frightened Miley.

"Since he saved me from going through the portal to the underworld," Miley replied. She couldn't believe this was happening! "Those kind of things make you realize what's important in life."

Lilly didn't buy it. "But ever since the day he got here, all I've heard from you is, 'Oh, he's so stuck up,' and 'Oh, who does he think he is?'"

"Yeah, well, I changed my mind."

Lilly's suspicions were growing. "Yeah,

right after he asked *me*," she said accus-
ingly.

"No!" Miley protested. "Actually, last
night. Which you would've known if you'd
had your mobile. *Photosynthesis?!* I mean,
come on!"

"How is this my fault?" Lilly asked.

Miley knew it wasn't really Lilly's fault.
But liking Jake wasn't her fault, either.
She saw only one solution. "Just tell him
you can't go to the dance and everything
will be fine," she told Lilly.

Lilly wasn't backing down. "But I don't
want to tell him that."

"But he likes me." Miley hated to break
it to Lilly, but she seemed to require a
reality check. "He only asked you because
I said no."

Lilly's eyes filled with tears and her voice
got resentful as she blasted Miley. "So what

are you saying? That I'm the tinned fruit you get when they're all out of the chocolate pudding?"

Lilly had thrown her. "What?" Miley had no idea how to respond.

"You know what I mean!" Lilly cried. "Well, I've got news for you: the Jake ship has sailed. And you're not on it!"

In the history of their friendship, Miley didn't think she'd ever seen Lilly this furious. And the fact that she was the cause of Lilly's fury made it that much worse.

Chapter Seven

Was it really morning already? Jackson didn't even open his eyes as his hand made the familiar motion towards the alarm clock on the bedside table. He slapped the OFF button with the palm of his hand and yawned. A warm breeze grazed his cheeks, as the lapping waves lulled him back to sleep. . . . It was so calming, so peaceful, so . . .

Warm breeze? Lapping waves? Jackson's eyes popped open. He gaped at the world around him. He was in his bed, but he wasn't in his bedroom. He was . . . he was . . . on the beach?!

Was he dreaming?

But then he heard the sound of trainers slapping sand. He turned to see his father approach. Mr Stewart was wearing a track suit and a wicked grin.

"Mornin', son," he greeted a still-groggy Jackson. "You sure are a heavy sleeper."

A couple of onlookers giggled. Jackson grimaced. "I'm gonna get you for this," he called out as his dad jogged past. Already his mind was racing with revenge schemes! He'd have to think of something good, *really* good.

When he threw off the covers, he got another shock. He was dressed in footie pyjamas – like a giant baby! He pulled the covers back over him.

His dad was better than good – he was awesome.

Chapter Eight

At first Miley and Lilly hadn't been thrilled about the idea of a seventies-themed dance. The seventies were just so . . . *old*. Miley's dad was always talking about how incredible they were. He *still* stayed up late at night watching the TV show reruns from back then. He'd sit on the couch, alternately stuffing his face with cheese snacks and chocolate-covered peanuts, laughing and shaking his head woefully as he moaned about how much cooler life used to be. Miley didn't really get it. On the TV shows her dad watched, they said these supercorny things like "jive turkey!" and "foxy!" On one show there was even a gang called the Sweathogs. Cool? Not so much.

In the end, the girls decided that the clothes from the seventies were cute, the hair-styles were pretty awesome and disco *was* good dance music.

Thinking it would snare him dates, Oliver had agreed to deejay the dance. Wearing a giant black wig and a shirt open down to his navel, Oliver played records from a booth overlooking the decked-out gym. "That was the Miami Funk Corporation with 'The Groove Is Gonna Getcha, Shoogie Oogie Oogie,'" he announced in a deep-throated

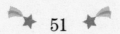

voice no one had heard him use before.

Lilly had been practising her seventies-style dance moves all day and now she was putting them to use with Jake. She still couldn't believe he'd asked her to the dance! "I'm having a great time," she said, swooning.

"Me, too," Jake answered noncommittally, his eye on the deejay booth. "Hey, you know, that reminds me. There's something I've been wanting to do all night."

Lilly had been thinking about kissing Jake all night. Well, actually, she'd been thinking about kissing Jake since the moment he'd asked her out. So, when he said there was something he'd wanted to do all night, she immediately jumped to the conclusion that he'd been thinking what she'd been thinking. "Really? Oh, boy!" She gasped dreamily. She closed her eyes tight and puckered up.

She waited. . . .

And waited. . . .

Sheesh! He was really taking his sweet time!

Finally, she opened her eyes to discover that Jake had vanished. Standing before her was a kid she barely knew. "Uh, just stretching my lips," she lied. "I heard the punch is tart."

Jake had made his way to the booth. "Hey, disco man," he greeted Oliver. "Mind if I borrow your mic?"

Oliver might try to play it cool, but even he was a little starstruck around Jake Ryan. "Dude, are you kidding?" he exclaimed. "Just let me do a quick intro." He put his lips to the microphone. "All you superfly guys and you foxy ladies, it gives me great pleasure to introduce a living legend, a star for the ages, the king of Funkytown –"

"Yo, Oliver." Jake finally interrupted. "Before the term ends."

"And my close personal friend, Jake Ryan . . ." Oliver looked like he was about to hand off the mic to Jake, except he took it back to say one last thing: ". . . who said I'm the second coolest guy at this school." he added.

"Thanks, everybody," Jake said as the students applauded. "I just want to say how happy I am to be part of a school where everybody is so nice . . . and alive." The crowd laughed; they were all *Zombie High* fans, after all. "Anyway, I want to dedicate this song to all the friends I've made here and . . . one very special friend. . . ." At the words "special friend," he looked straight at Lilly.

She looked like she might melt. Life had never been so perfect!

That is, until Miley walked in to spoil it! She was wearing a supercute red dress and seemed all too aware that all eyes were now on her. "Hey y'all! What's up?" she yelled.

Jake was still at the microphone. It took him a second to catch his breath. "Whoa," was all he could muster.

Lilly's moment was ruined. And by her best friend! Scratch that! Her soon-to-be-*ex*-best friend! She made a beeline for Miley and got straight to the accusations. "What are you doing?" She looked Miley up and down. Did Miley have to look so out-of-control terrific?

Proving she could indeed act, Miley put on her most innocent voice. "Oh, my goodness!" She gasped. "I completely forgot. I hope I don't stand out."

Lilly wasn't having any of it. "I know exactly what you're doing. You're trying to get Jake to notice you."

Miley wasn't going to drop the act. "No, I'm not," she replied. Out of the corner of her eye she saw Jake. "Oh. Hi!" she called out, using her sweetest possible voice.

"Hi, Miley," Jake said. "You look great."

"Really?" Lilly seethed. "I think she looks like a fire engine."

But Jake was smitten. He corrected Lilly. "A very cute fire engine," he told her.

Lilly could feel the rage travel from her toes to her fingertips. If she had to stand there any longer watching Jake make goo-goo eyes at Miley . . . well, she didn't know what she'd do! "Hey, less talkie, more dancie," she ordered, dragging Jake away. "Oliver!" she called out. "Let's get this party started! Now!"

Miley watched Lilly and Jake, feeling more determined than ever. After all, she hadn't got gussied up for nothing! Miley had pulled some serious favours from Hannah Montana's stylists to score the amazing red dress. She'd exfoliated, she'd moisturized, she'd plucked and primped. She'd crammed her feet into heels that were way too tight. She was going to be sporting some wickedly massive blisters tomorrow – and they'd better be worth it.

Miley grabbed a kid she barely knew and danced over to Lilly and Jake. She shook her hair from side to side and swivelled her hips until Jake noticed her. She smiled sweetly, wondering if she should ask to cut in. It'd be bold, but it would probably work. . . .

Should I do it? Miley thought. Lilly would be so mad. Well, so what? Jake liked me! He'd told me so. Well, okay, he'd told Hannah Montana. But, still! She was mulling her options when *thud!* Something slammed into her hip. *Ouch!* She lurched sideways, teetering on her tight heels. Who was the giant klutz with two left feet?

She turned to discover . . . it was Lilly! And she hadn't just tripped. She'd slammed into her. On purpose. Well! Miley had no option but to bump right back. She flung her hip towards Lilly's and sent her flying. Now, not only was she going to have blisters tomorrow . . . she was going to be black-and-blue.

Oliver noticed the commotion from the deejay booth. "Looks like somebody's trying to bump up the party!" he announced. "Everybody's doing the bump."

But Jake could tell this was more than just a dance. "Girls, please put the claws away," he said.

"Stay out of this, Jake!" Lilly screeched.

"Yeah, we're fighting over you!" Miley shouted.

This made Lilly even madder. "Knock it off, he's my date!"

Bump!

"He asked me first!" Miley snapped.

Bump!

"You said 'no' three times!" Lilly yelled. "Forgive me for thinking that meant 'no.'"

Bump!

"You're forgiven," Miley said, very sarcastically.

Bump!

The other dancers misconstrued Lilly and Miley's increasingly volatile argument as a call to bump one another even harder. Soon, bodies were careening across the room.

Meanwhile, Miley and Lilly each took hold of one of Jake's arms as if he were a giant wishbone. "Ouch! Celebrity in pain!" he cried unhappily.

Jake didn't need to use even half his strength to wriggle free. He was The Zombie Slayer, after all. He flapped his arms twice, sending Lilly and Miley sailing across the room in opposite directions.

Lilly smashed into the table with the punch bowl, while Miley hit the one with the appetizers.

Chapter Nine

Funny that only a few days ago Miley and Lilly had been hanging out in the toilets joking about Jake Ryan. Now, they were standing before the very same mirrors fighting over him.

Miley picked the insides of a soggy egg roll out of her hair as Lilly wrung the punch out of her wig. "Congratulations," Lilly said, scowling at Miley. "You made me look ridiculous in front of Jake."

Miley shook the tortilla chips off the front of her dress. "Well, look what you did to me," she replied.

"Hey, I'm not the one who tried to steal someone else's date. How could you do that to me?"

It was strange. In the day since Jake had asked Lilly out, Miley had felt wronged and misunderstood. All she'd wanted was to get what she deserved, which in her mind was Jake.

Miley still felt that way. But now, looking at Lilly drenched in punch, with a devastated look in her eyes, Miley wondered how worth it Jake could be. She and Lilly had sworn up and down never to let a guy come between them.

"I don't know!" Miley cried. "It was just Jake and . . . he's just so cute . . . and that thunder mint . . . wow, and I kissed a dog. I think I deserve it!"

Lilly looked at her, considering. "Well, you can have him," she said finally. "I don't like him that much anyway."

One of the things Miley loved most about Lilly was that she always did the unexpected. Still, she *really* hadn't been expecting this.

"Since when?" Miley asked.

"Since . . ." Lilly thought about it for a second. "Since I saw the way he looked at you," she admitted.

Miley knew it! Jake did only have eyes for her! But hearing Lilly say so didn't feel as good as she'd thought it would. "Lilly, I –" Miley was at a loss for words.

"Forget it," Lilly said. "Easy come, easy go. Now go back out there. I'll just rinse the sorbet out of my wig."

Miley had won, but, she wasn't sure if

she could leave Lilly. As much as Miley wanted to get back to Jake, she needed to know things were right with Lilly. "You gonna be okay?" she asked.

"Yeah, I'm fine," Lilly said, choking back a tear.

"Lilly!" Miley could feel a tear coming herself.

"It's nothing," Lilly said with a sniffle. "I'm just rinsing my wig . . . with my tears."

Miley couldn't bear it. Forget the dance. Forget Jake.

"Why aren't you leaving?" Lilly asked.

Miley watched the orange sorbet from the punch bowl swirl in the sink, thinking she'd do anything to go back in time and not have fought with Lilly. "Because I hurt my best friend over some guy," she said. Now, she was crying, too. "And nobody, not even Jake Ryan, is worth that. I'm sorry, Lilly."

Lilly turned to face Miley. Now both of their faces were streaked with mascara and tears. "You should be," Lilly said. They hugged – a sticky, punch-covered, greasy appetizer hug.

"You smell really bad," Miley told Lilly.

"You smell really bad, too," Lilly replied.

Miley grinned, knowing Lilly meant it in the best possible way.

Chapter Ten

Jackson and his father sat on the couch watching TV. What should have been an exercise in relaxed couch potatodom was anything but. Every time one of them reached for the remote or the bowl of popcorn, the other flinched, thinking they were about to be pranked.

"Hey, Jackson, get up and get me a drink, would ya?" Mr Stewart asked.

Jackson rolled his eyes. How gullible did his dad think he was? "Yeah, sure," he said sarcastically. "I go and open the refrigerator and a monkey pops out and hits me over the head with a banana." He didn't mean to be disrespectful to his dad, but war was war. "You want a drink," he told Mr Stewart, "you go and get it."

But Mr Stewart was the wiser of the two! He wasn't budging. "Oh, no, I see what you're doing. Turn it around so I get up and open up the refrigerator and the monkey hits me in the face with a pie."

"Aha!" Jackson exclaimed. "So there is a monkey."

It was going to be a long weekend. . . .

Meanwhile, the dance at Seaview Middle School was still going strong.

"Hey, you two okay?" Jake asked when

Lilly and Miley finally emerged.

"Yeah," answered Lilly, "we're fine."

"We talked. We worked it all out," Miley told him.

"Sorry, Jake," Lilly said. "I'm not into you any more."

Jake took the rejection in his stride. "That's cool," he said, before turning to Miley. "You wanna dance?" he asked.

Miley didn't pause – not for a second – before letting Jake down. "No thanks. I'm gonna dance with my best friend." She grabbed Lilly by the elbow and pulled her onto the dance floor, ready to get down and boogie.

Jake had no shortage of admirers, so he wasn't dancing by himself for long. "I don't know what they see in him," Lilly remarked as she and Miley watched the girls clamour around him.

"Neither do I," Miley agreed. The disco music blared all around them. She watched Jake do the hustle. Boy, he's a good dancer, she thought. He caught her looking at him from across the room. She remembered how blue his eyes were. They looked even bluer under the rotating disco ball…. Miley sighed.

"Good thing we're over him," Lilly said with a wink.

Miley turned her attention back to her best friend. "Oh, yeah," she finally said.

Together, they danced the night away.

"I wasn't nervous then. I'm not nervous now," Miley said. "I just don't want to go to the dance with you."

"First, this girl I like won't go to the school dance with me, and now my zombie princess won't kiss me," Jake said.

Jake really is cute, Miley thought. And he thinks
I'm cute . . . and down to earth. Oh, stop it, Miley.
You don't like him.

As Mr. Stewart gasped in horror, Jackson let out
a triumphant "Booyah!"

"I should move on, I know," Jake said. "That's why
I came over here to ask Lilly."

"Girls, please put the claws away," Jake said.

"I see what you're doing," Mr. Stewart said. "Turn it around so the monkey hits me in the face with a pie."

"No, thanks. I'm gonna dance with my best friend," Miley told Jake.

"If we'd been able to finish our kiss on *Zombie High*, we might've won this thing," Jake announced.

"I'm home-schooled. In Canada. Where the moose are," said Lilly, who was dressed as Lola.

"That could have been you over there givin' Jake little popcorn kissies," Lilly told Miley.

"Oh, hi, Jake. I didn't notice you here on the beach," Miley lied.

"Dad, the weirdest thing happened at school today," Jackson announced.

"No, that kid just looks like him . . . and has the same name . . . and knows me," Miley said.

"What's a dash of tarragon between friends?"
asked Jackson.

"I already admitted I was wrong. You don't have
to blow my nose in it," said Miley.

PART TWO

Chapter One

It took a lot for Hannah Montana to get nervous. But as she stood on-stage next to the totally hot heartthrob Jake Ryan, she was flustered, discombobulated and rattled. She was also freaked out, twitchy and jumpy.

After all, Jake Ryan was . . . well, he was so many things. He was her co-star (at least for an episode) on *Zombie High*, whom she'd come *this close* to kissing. And he was also her classmate, who at first had seemed ridiculously self-centred but turned out to be totally sweet and genuine. After all, he'd admitted he liked her – and not the *Hannah Montana* her, but the *Miley* her. He was also the cause of her biggest, ugliest fight with her best friend, Lilly. Thankfully, she and Lilly had made up. Still, Miley hadn't stopped thinking about Jake since, even though enough time had passed for him to start dating some other girl at school.

So when Miley had learned he'd be Hannah Montana's co-presenter at the Teen Scene Awards, she'd been superpsyched. And when she had found out they'd be presenting the award for Best On-screen Kiss, she couldn't believe her luck. It was so perfect and *so* romantic!

Yet, now, as the crowd of teenagers stared at her expectantly and the hot fluorescent lights beamed down on her, all her enthusiasm was causing her to sweat uncontrollably. She was holding the envelope with the name of the winner inside and it was getting soggier by the second. If they didn't get to it quick, Miley worried the winner's name would get smudged. Then it would be unreadable and they wouldn't know who'd won – all because of her relentless sweating. She'd have to admit it on live television. It would be in all the tabloids that week, not to mention the gossip blogs. It was all too horrifying to think about!

Miley's head was spinning. Meanwhile, the teleprompter glared menacingly at her. Oh, yeah, her line. *Stop thinking about sweat, Miley!* she told herself. Speak!

"Those are your nominees for Best On-screen Kiss. And the Teenie Award

goes to . . ." She hoped her voice didn't sound too shaky.

As with all award shows, their lines featured witty banter that was supposed to seem spontaneous. "You know," Jake said, smirking slightly at Miley, "if we'd been able to finish our kiss on *Zombie High*, we might've won this thing."

Miley thought back to their almost kiss: how he'd held her in his arms. His *strong, strong* arms! How his face had been so close to hers. How she'd been able to smell the thunder-mint breath spray. How she could smell it again now. . . .

She was staring adoringly at him, when he nudged her. "Your turn," he reminded her.

"Oh, right!" Miley couldn't believe this. What was happening to her? She looked at the teleprompter for guidance. "Oh, Jake," she cooed. "I bet you say that to all your co-stars," she read. The crowd laughed. Phew, she was doing okay now.

The teleprompter also gave stage directions. PUSH JAKE, it said now. "Push Jake," Miley read. *Push Jake? What? Oh!* "I mean –," she stumbled, trying to recover while giving Jake's arm – *his strong, strong arm!* – a little push. "And the Teenie for Best On-screen Kiss goes to . . ." She opened the envelope. Phew, not too soggy, she thought. ". . . Frankie Muniz and his pillow in *The Lonely Sophomore*. Good job, Frankie!"

"Unfortunately, Frankie's doing a movie in Romania," Jake told the crowd.

Now it was Miley's turn to be witty. "And the pillow had a hot date with a bunk bed, hold for laughter." *Hold for laughter?* Oh, no, she'd read the stage directions out loud . . . again.

"We'll be accepting this on Frankie's behalf," Jake told the applauding crowd. The music swelled as Miley and Jake began their walk off the stage. "Thank you!" Miley called out. "And, oh, next year I promise I'll do better." She waved to the audience, shouting, "Toodles!"

She'd never been so happy to get out of the limelight.

Backstage was a chaotic mess of producers, stagehands and teen stars waiting in the wings. Still, it was calm compared to being on-stage. Once they were behind the curtains, Miley let out her frustrations. "*Ahhhhhh!* Man! Darn-it!" she cried.

Jake did his best to comfort her. "Come on. People love it when we mess up. Besides, I think you did great."

Miley appreciated Jake's attempt to

console her, but seriously, who was he kidding? Her hideous performance was looping through her head on fast-forward. "Thanks, hold for applause," she replied with a grimace.

Jake laughed good-naturedly. "Great to see you again, Hannah. Can't wait to get you back on the show to finish that kiss. I'll have my people call your people."

"Great," Miley answered. Sometimes show business-speak cracked her up. *My people.* "My people will be waiting," she replied.

"That would be me!" called an all-too-eager voice. It belonged to Lilly in disguise as Hannah Montana's right-hand gal, Lola Luftnagle. "I'm Lola, her most important people," Lilly chirped nervously. "Which is why I may look familiar, but we've never met. Not even in school or anything. 'Cause

I'm home-schooled. In Canada. Where the moose are."

Apparently Miley wasn't the only one flustered by Jake Ryan's presence. Lilly was acting more than a little loopy.

"*Ohh*-kay," Jake told Lola (aka Lilly) politely. "Nice to meet you, too. Bye." He then bid a hasty retreat; Miley couldn't blame him.

"Where the moose are?" she teased Lilly. "In Canada? Where I'm home-schooled. Lola, way to keep your cover."

Lilly shrugged. She might have acted nutty, but she really was over Jake. "Oh, who cares? Hey, you know what? I heard he broke up with that girl at school."

It was rare that Jake was single, so Miley recognized how huge this opportunity was. "I can't wait to go to school on Monday!" she told Lilly. "Maybe Jake and I can finally get together."

They heard a commotion coming from stage left. Miley turned to see a circle of photographers surrounding a couple. She squinted past the glare of flashbulbs to see who it was. First she saw the girl: it was Holly Shannon, the It-actress of the moment. But what guy was she dating?

Miley heard the photographers call Jake's name and then Miley realized: the guy next to Holly Shannon was none other than Jake Ryan. *Her* Jake Ryan! For someone newly single, the guy sure worked fast!

"Sorry," said Lilly.

Miley hadn't thought her night could get worse! "No, I'm fine with it," she lied through gritted teeth. "I'm cool. I'm really, really fine."

Snap!

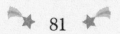

Miley looked down. She hadn't real-ized she was still holding Frankie Muniz's uncollected Teenie Award. In her anger, she'd broken off the statue's head. "Oops," she said.

She was fine. Really, she was.

Chapter Two

Miley had barely recovered from the shock of seeing Jake with Holly, when she came in contact with the couple again.

It was the morning after the Teen Scene Awards and she'd gone to Rico's to meet Lilly. The two girls were innocently taking in the sun and eating ice-cream cones, when they spied Jake and Holly, this time getting cosy by the snack bar. Yet again, they were surrounded by a group of photographers.

"Okay, you've got enough shots," Jake told the paparazzi. "Can we have a little privacy now? Thanks." Miley watched in disgust as Jake and Holly started to feed each other like a newly married couple sharing their first bite of wedding cake. Boy, they thought they were cute! And were those matching sunglasses? Miley thought she might puke from all the lovey-doveyness.

Meanwhile, she'd taken her rage out on the ice-cream cone in her hand, which she had crushed in her clenched fist. Melted ice cream oozed through her fingers.

Lilly looked down at the ice cream and remarked, "Wow! First the Teenie, now this. You've got it bad."

There was no hiding it. "I know," Miley woefully confessed.

"And what's worse is Jake liked you first and you turned him down."

Lilly didn't have to remind her! Rarely did a day go by when Miley didn't think about how much she'd messed up with Jake. When he'd liked her, she'd rejected him for being an egomaniac. But by the time she'd figured out he was really a decent guy, he'd moved on to Lilly, of all people. That had led to a big fight between Miley and Lilly, but they had finally decided that their friendship was worth more than a guy — even when that guy was Jake.

Still, Miley couldn't help feeling a pang of regret as she and Lilly watched Jake and Holly cuddling. It was a scene right out of a horror movie — so gross, except you couldn't take your eyes off it. "That could have been you over there givin' Jake little popcorn kissies," Lilly said.

Now Lilly was *trying* to needle her. "Oh,

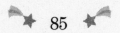

Lilly, you've got a bit of ice cream on your face," Miley teased.

"Where?" Lilly asked.

Miley took Lilly's cone and planted it on her nose.

"Right there," she replied, giggling.

"Thanks." Lilly tried to sniff, but ice cream clogged her nostrils.

Just then, a guy they didn't recognize approached. "Hey, need a napkin?" he asked.

What kind of freak goes around offering girls napkins? Miley wondered. Then, out of the corner of her eye, she noticed that Jake was watching her. Watching her talk to a guy – a freaky napkin-offering guy, but still a guy. . . .

Miley took another look at the stranger. He was cute in a baby-faced kind of way. Cute enough, at least. "You know," Miley said in her flirtiest voice, "a girl can never have too many napkins." She took one. "Thanks," she said, introducing herself. "I'm Miley."

"I'm Willis," said the guy.

Miley could hear Jake and Holly cooing. She glanced over to see if Jake was watching her; sure enough, he was. She turned it up a notch. "You're so funny, so funny," she told Willis, making sure to laugh louder than Jake and Holly. "Here, take a seat. You come here often?"

"No. I just moved from Seattle."

She'd have thought she'd captured Jake's attention by now. But he was still paying attention to that horrible Holly. Miley was going to have to work even harder. "Seattle!" she hooted as if Willis had just said something hilarious. "There is no stopping you now, is there?"

 87

Poor Willis looked to Lilly for help. "I don't get it either," she said with a shrug.

"So where are you going to school?" Miley asked him.

"Eastwood Prep. But I'm graduating."

"You're a senior?!" Lilly exclaimed. "'Cause we're just —"

"Starving!" Miley blurted out. She was thankful to have interrupted Lilly before she'd spilled their secret. A senior! This changed everything! "Why don't I go get us all some pretzels?" Miley suggested. "Wait here, Walter."

"It's Willis," he corrected her.

"Still so funny!" Miley said, with a fake laugh. "You just keep on killing me!" She turned to Lilly and whispered, "Make sure he doesn't go anywhere."

"What are you doing?" Lilly gasped.

"You can't flirt with a senior? He's old enough to –"

"Make Jake jealous?" Miley said. "So he'll realize I'm the girl he really wants?"

Finally, Lilly was catching on. "Ooooh, diabolical!" she cried. "Or should I say '*guy*-abolical'?"

It wasn't like Miley to play games. She usually liked to be straightforward. In the back of her mind, she knew the right thing to do was to be honest. She should tell Jake how she felt and ask him out. But that would be a risk. Miley really liked him and if he rejected her . . . well, it would really hurt. Playing games was a lot safer. For Miley, that is.

Nervous energy travelled through Miley's limbs, as she sauntered over to the snack bar for the pretzels she'd pretended to want. She took a deep breath, then shook her hair from side to side so it had that perfect blowing-in-the-wind beach look. "Oh, hi, Jake," she said, careful to sound oh-so-casual. "I didn't notice you here on the beach," she lied.

Jake lied back. "Oh, hey, Miley. I didn't notice you here on the beach, either." He introduced Holly, explaining, "She's an actress." Where does he think I live? Miley wondered. Under a rock? Like he needs to introduce her.

"So, who's your friend?" Jake asked.

"Oh, that's Willis," Miley said, as if it were an everyday event that she met cute, new *older* guys. "He's from Seattle, the coffee capital of America. He drinks it . . . black."

If Jake was impressed, he didn't show it. "Holly drinks espresso," he said.

"Willis is a senior," Miley said, dealing the final blow.

Thud.

Finally, something had worked! Before Jake could formulate a comeback, Miley had turned to leave. "Toodles!" she cried cheerily, feeling awfully proud.

Miley delivered the pretzels to Lilly and Willis. "Hey," said Willis, "I was wondering if maybe you wanted to go to this bowling party with me?"

Miley couldn't believe how well this was going! She'd trumped Jake and now she was being asked out by a senior. Okay, she didn't feel the same way about him as she felt about Jake, but that didn't matter. What mattered was that Jake would be superjealous.

"Sure," she said loud enough for Jake

to hear. "Of course I'll go to the bowling party with you. With all of your senior classmates." She practically screamed the words *senior classmates*.

Miley couldn't help sneaking a peek at Jake and Holly. Had she got a reaction from them? She was pretty sure the answer was yes, because Jake was practically throwing popcorn down poor Holly's throat, shouting "Oh, Holly! Open up."

Gosh, thought Miley, some people are so obvious.

Chapter Three

Mr Stewart was heading out of the front door when Jackson caught up with him. He was surprised to see Jackson, whom he considered the more uncomplicated of his two children, looking so jittery and pale-faced. Then again, Mr Stewart was on his way to his son's parent-teacher conference. And Jackson wasn't known for his stellar school record – especially where behaviour was concerned.

"Okay, Dad, you may hear a little something about a belching contest," Jackson said. "I just want you to know that it never happened. And I was not the champion."

Mr Stewart was no stranger to his son's childish ways. Not only that . . . when it came to Jackson's immature streak, it was really a case of "like father, like son."

"I can't say I approve of that kind of behaviour," Mr Stewart remarked. "But I guess better out of the attic than out of the basement."

Jackson laughed, looking relieved. "Thanks," he said, "but don't try that kind of humour with Ms Kunkle," he warned. "She doesn't have a funny bone in her body."

Mr Stewart had heard Jackson's tales of woe involving the humourless Ms Kunkle, but he didn't buy them. "I bet I'll get a giggle out of her," Mr Stewart said with a swagger. "I know she hasn't heard this one: Knock-knock –"

Jackson looked aghast. "No, no, no Dad! No, no, no 'knock-knock' jokes! No jokes at all! If you even think something funny, I'm gonna get detention!"

His son sure had a flair for the dramatic! "Stop exaggerating," Mr Stewart told him. "No one who dedicates themselves to a life of educating kids could be that mean."

Jackson looked at him like he had no idea. . . .

Chapter Four

Lilly was adamant. "You can't go out with this guy," she told Miley the next day at school. "You start bowling with a senior, the next thing you know, you're go-karting with a college guy! It's madness!"

Miley took Lilly's hysteria in her stride. "Hey, who sprinkled 'drama queen' in your oatmeal this morning?" she asked Lilly. "Relax. I was never really gonna go out with Willis. I just said it to make Jake jealous."

"So how are you going to get out of the bowling party?" her friend Oliver asked. Lilly had told Oliver about the whole Willis-Jake drama.

Did her friends have no faith? Miley had already come up with an excuse – she'd even got pretty creative. "I'll just call Willis and tell him that I totally forgot I'm allergic to rental shoes. Perfect."

"Hey, guys!" called a familiar voice. It was Jake. He turned to Miley and gave her a smirk. "So I guess I'll see you at the bowling alley tonight," he said.

Miley was trying to act as cool and nonchalant as ever. "Yeah, that sounds –" she started. *"What?!"*

"Well," remarked Jake, "I just thought that Holly and I would have a great time bowling, too. So we'll probably bump into you there."

Miley hadn't been expecting this. Time to think quick. "I'm sure you would," she replied, "but I'm not sure if I'm still gonna. . . ."

"Oh, did your senior boyfriend already break up with you?" Jake asked, sounding a little too self-satisfied for Miley's tastes.

Didn't he wish! "No!" Miley protested. "I'm just not sure if . . ." She had to think of something! But she couldn't think of anything! *Ack!* ". . . I'm wearing my red top or my green, just in case you're looking for me."

Jake looked sceptical, but also a little disappointed. "Thanks for being so thoughtful," he said.

"My pleasure," she cooed.

Once Jake was gone, Miley waved off Lilly's and Oliver's looks of concern. "I've got him just where I want him," she assured them.

They looked as doubtful as she felt.

Chapter Five

Jackson had been asleep when Mr Stewart had returned from the parent-teacher conference the previous night, and then Mr Stewart had been out jogging when Jackson had been getting ready for school the next morning. So they hadn't had a chance to talk about what had happened with Ms Kunkle.

At three pm, Jackson arrived home from school. He was brimming with news. "Dad, the weirdest thing happened at school today!" he announced. "I think Ms Kunkle actually smiled."

"Is that so?" Mr Stewart tried not to sound smug. He'd decided he was going to play it cool.

"Yeah, some people said it was a trick of the light and I had my money on a gas bubble. Did she seem okay when you talked to her last night?" Jackson asked.

"Karen?" Mr Stewart said, acting like calling Ms Kunkle by her first name was a perfectly normal thing to do. "Yeah, she seemed fine. And later at coffee –"

It took several seconds for Jackson to process this information. Later. At. Coffee. "W-w-w-whoa!" he exclaimed. "You and Kunkle had coffee? You're kidding!"

"And an apple crumble," Mr Stewart said casually.

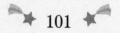

"I can't believe it!" Jackson gasped. "And now Ms Kunkle is – smiling."

That should show Jackson not to doubt his old man! "Really?" Mr Stewart was really working the blasé act. "I didn't do anything but talk with her. And I was havin' a pretty good hair day."

Jackson stood silently, taking it all in. "Wait a minute," he reflected. "If after a half hour with you and your hair she's smiling, imagine what she'd be like after a real date with you." He paused for a moment, as if in a reverie, imagining all the possibilities: His dad and Ms Kunkle . . . Ms Kunkle and his dad . . . His dad would be happy, Ms Kunkle would be happy. Shoot, he'd never been a teacher's pet before. He'd probably get an A in her class. Who knew his old dad had it in him? Props to Pops!

"So when are you gonna see her again?" he asked finally.

"We never talked about it."

Jackson didn't like the sound of that! He grabbed the phone and dialled the school. As someone who was known to crank-call the principal's office on occasion, he knew the number by heart. "Well, get on it, Romeo! It's time to runkle with the –" The receptionist picked up. Jackson turned on his phone voice. "Karen Kunkle, please."

Mr Stewart lurched for the phone. What did his son think he was doing? "But, Jackson, don't you dare –" he sputtered. It was too late. Jackson held the phone up to Mr Stewart's ear. "Uh, hello, Karen," Mr Stewart fumbled, glaring evilly at Jackson. "Yeah, this is Robby Stewart. . . ."

Jackson ignored his father's anger.

"Work it, Dad, work it," he whispered encouragingly.

Jackson's life had suddenly taken a turn for the awesome.

Chapter Six

The bowling alley was the last place that Lilly and Oliver wanted to spend a weekend night, a fact they kept telling Miley over and over – and over – again. She'd had to promise about a zillion favours to get them to come. Tonight better be worth it, because Miley was going to be mowing Lilly's lawn and cleaning the inside of Oliver's locker from now until the end of the next school year.

"I've got a bad feeling about this," Lilly said with a groan as they entered Parkway Lanes. Her ominous tone clashed with the bowling alley's bright and colourful decor.

"Come on, we'll just stay long enough for Jake to see me with Willis and then we'll be out of here," Miley told her. Meanwhile, she looked around for signs of Willis and his senior buddies or Jake and Holly. She didn't see anyone – just a bunch of guys from the bowling league and a group of little kids who were having a party. Oh, cute! They were wearing balloon hats! Miley hadn't seen a balloon hat in forever.

"I don't see Willis," Oliver remarked.

"Just look for a bunch of cool, older guys," Miley said.

As soon as the words *cool, older guys* left

her lips, Miley noticed two kids coming towards her. Both were wearing balloon hats. At first she worried that they'd somehow recognized her as Hannah Montana – after all, she had a huge fan base among elementary school kids. But then she was shocked when one of them greeted her by her name – her real name. "Hey, Miley! Hi!" She was even more shocked when she realized that the kid speaking to her was none other than . . . *Willis*.

Funny how young Willis looked in the company of another young kid! Miley guessed it was probably his little brother or cousin. "Hey, Willis. Who's this?"

"My best friend," Willis answered.

Well, that was sweet. He called his little brother – or cousin – his best friend. Willis turned to the boy. "Mike, this is that girl I was telling you about. What do you think?"

Miley stood there uncomfortably as Mike looked her up and down. "Hubba-hubba," he proclaimed before blushing madly and running off.

Well, thought Miley, that was kind of sweet, but also a little gross.

Miley expected Willis to explain who the kid was, but he just stood there grinning. "How old is he?" Miley asked finally.

"I know, I know, he looks ten," Willis explained, "but he's really twelve."

Oh. Well. Huh? "Isn't it weird hanging around with guys so much younger than you?" Miley asked.

Willis stared at the floor for a couple of seconds looking bashful. "Well, truth is," he confessed, "Mike's older than me."

"How old are you?" Oliver asked. Miley was so stunned, she'd actually forgotten Lilly and Oliver were there.

"Eleven," Willis answered. "And three-quarters," he added brightly.

Eleven? As in one year older than ten and one year younger than twelve? "You're eleven?!" Miley cried.

"And three-quarters," Willis reminded her.

Well, thought Miley bitterly, that changes everything.

Chapter Seven

Who cared if the kid was eleven? He was a liar, a big fat liar, and Miley was going to call him on it. He'd totally played her! The little sneak!

"You said you were graduating!" she cried, wagging her finger threateningly.

"I am," Willis argued.

"Elementary school?!" Miley said incredulously. He'd meant he was graduating from elementary school! The nerve of this kid!

"Sorry," Willis said. "I thought it'd be cool to be at the party with, you know, an older babe."

So that's why he'd done it? To impress his friends and look cool. Boy, was that pathetic.

"I can't believe you used me!" Miley's head was spinning. She was going to get this kid. She should tell his parents. That would serve him right! But then Lilly brought her back to earth.

"You mean just like you used him?" she whispered in Miley's ear.

Oh, Miley thought. Lilly did have a point.

"Okay, fine," Miley conceded. "I used him. It was wrong. I learned my lesson and I'll never do it again."

Just then, Oliver noticed Jake and Holly on their way to the shoe-rental counter.

"Jake alert," he warned Miley.

Oh, no! Without thinking, Miley grabbed Willis. She'd stop using people, really she would . . . just right after this. "Quick, put your arm around me," she commanded, grabbing Willis's arm and twisting him around so their backs were to Jake and Holly.

"Wow!" Willis gasped in awe. "I'm touching shoulder."

Miley tried to stay calm. If they could just stand like this, without Jake and Holly seeing, she could save face. But then Willis's little friend, Mike, came skipping over. "Willis, come on. They're cutting the cake!" he announced. "It's shaped like a castle!"

"In a minute," Willis told him.

Good boy, Miley thought.

"Well, you better hurry if you want any

of the pudding moat," Mike cautioned.

Unfortunately for Miley, the words "pudding moat" were too much for someone who was eleven and three-quarters. Before she knew it, he'd ditched her. Oliver, always a sucker for a good pudding moat, couldn't help but follow.

Now what was she going to do? Miley grabbed a bowling ball to shield her face. "All right, Lilly, come on," she whispered. "Let's get out of here before Jake —"

But it was too late. Jake and Holly were on their way over. Even from behind the bowling ball, Miley could see they were holding hands. "Isn't that your senior boyfriend over there?" Holly asked, pointing to the kids' birthday party, where a balloon-sword fight was under way.

"No, that kid just looks like him," Miley lied.

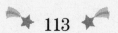

"I am King Willis!" they heard Willis shout.

"And has the same name," she added.

Just then, Willis spotted Miley looking at him. "Hi, Miley!" he called.

"And knows me," she added meekly.

Chapter Eight

Jackson was confused. It smelled like his dad was cooking gumbo. Mr Stewart only cooked gumbo on special occasions, like Thanksgiving and Christmas. Was today a holiday?

"Dad, what are you doing?" Jackson asked as he entered the kitchen. Mr Stewart was peering into a pot.

"What does it look like I'm doing?" Mr Stewart's face was red from the steaming pot – or maybe that was anger upon see-ing Jackson. "Thanks to you, I'm cooking Chicken à la Kunkle."

It didn't seem like his dad would appre-ciate it, so Jackson kept his delight to himself. Ms Kunkle was coming over! He was one step closer to the good life! Easy A's and no detention!

Then again, his dad could blow it at the last second. No matter how suave he thought he was, Mr Stewart could be a lit-tle thick when it came to the ladies. Jackson took it upon himself to intervene.

First, his dad's outfit: the dude was wear-ing an apron. An apron! Jackson hated to break it to his dad, but it was for his own good. "You can't have a woman over for a date lookin' like you just got off the late shift at the Waffle Wagon."

Mr Stewart rolled his eyes. "It's not a

date, Son. It's two adults havin' dinner because one adult's son hoodwinked him into it."

Jackson didn't know what *hoodwinked* meant and he didn't care. Just as long as his dad took off the apron before Ms Kunkle got there. They were so close; they couldn't afford any slip ups now.

Nothing was weirder than seeing a teacher out of the context of school. Except seeing her at your front door, that is.

The first thing Jackson noticed was that Ms Kunkle wasn't wearing her usual buttoned-up teacher attire. As he ushered her into the kitchen, he decided that Ms Kunkle actually looked like a normal person. Wait until he told Rico.

"'Orange' you a sight for sore eyes?" said Mr Stewart, holding up the orange in his hand, when he saw Ms Kunkle.

Oh, man, thought Jackson mournfully, this night is going to be over quickly if Dad doesn't cut out the lame puns.

Except Ms Kunkle lapped it up! "Robby, you are so *punny*!" she exclaimed, giggling. Ms Kunkle – the very same Ms Kunkle who gave the girls who sat in the back of class detention for giggling – was chuckling at his dad's bad jokes.

"Smells incredible," Ms Kunkle said, taking a deep breath.

"And it tastes even better!" Mr Stewart boasted. He dipped the spoon in the pot and offered her a taste.

Jackson watched as Ms Kunkle leaned in to taste Mr Stewart's gumbo, thinking he'd never got so lucky in his life. Ms Kunkle would always treat him well now: she'd probably excuse him from class whenever he wanted . . . give him extra time on tests . . . let him turn in homework late . . . or maybe not at all!

Crazy how in a flash, one stupid little remark, can change everything. "*Mmmmm, wonderful,*" Ms Kunkle said, licking her lips. But I think it could use just a dash of tarragon."

Uh-oh. No one criticized Mr Stewart's gumbo! Jackson held his breath waiting for his dad to respond. He prayed Mr Stewart would just let it go.

But then things got even worse when Ms Kunkle reached for the tarragon. She held it over the pot, poised to sprinkle.

Mr Stewart smashed a lid down on the pot before she got to it. The lid made an unpleasant clanging sound. "Whoa, whoa, whoa!" Mr Stewart cried. "We got a pretty delicate balance of spices here. Wouldn't want to throw it out of whack, but thanks for the thought."

His dad was being polite, but Jackson could tell it was forced. The guy was a total control freak when it came to cooking. "I'm just talking about a dash," Ms Kunkle said sweetly, adding, "I'm a pretty fair cook myself, you know."

Was Mr Stewart going to break? Jackson watched in fear as his dad inhaled sharply, doing his best to hold himself back. "That may be," he said in his most measured tone. "But this recipe's been in the family for generations."

Ms Kunkle wasn't getting the hint. "Well, that doesn't mean it can't be improved," she countered.

Mr Stewart took this as a personal insult. "It was good enough to take second place for Recipe of the Year at the Tennessee State Fair."

"Well, maybe if it had a dash of tarragon, it would've won," Ms Kunkle replied.

Jackson had to do something to diffuse the situation. "Hey, now, hey," he interrupted. "Let's not forget about the apple crumble. Good times, good times."

Apparently this was the wrong thing to say, because Ms Kunkle crinkled up her lips, remarking sourly, "Well, I remember the apple because someone else ate all the crumble."

Jackson had to admit: his dad could be a crumble hog.

"And it was delicious because it didn't have any tarragon in it," Mr Stewart shot back.

"Hey, hey." Jackson kept doing his best to mediate. "Who wants to get a pizza?

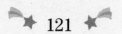

They actually put cheese in the crust now. *Mmmmmmm.*"

But Mr Stewart ignored Jackson. He just couldn't hold back anymore. "You know, everybody's entitled to their opinion," he told Ms Kunkle. "But in this case, yours is wronger than a monkey driving a lawn mower!"

Ms Kunkle stared at Mr Stewart disdainfully. Uh-oh. Jackson recognized that stare. It was the same stare she gave him before sending him to detention. "Well, my opinion can't be any *wronger* than your grammar, cowboy!"

Her cutting words hung heavily in the room. Jackson couldn't take the tension. "Oh, pshaw!" he exclaimed. "What's a dash of tarragon between friends?"

Apparently a dash was . . . a lot. Because at this point, his dad and Ms Kunkle were anything but friends. "Okay, that's it," Mr Stewart huffed. "The next one that says 'tarragon' is gonna be gone."

Ms Kunkle took this as a cue. "Tarragon . . . tarragon . . ." she repeated mockingly as she stomped towards the door. "I am so gone!"

"I'm sorry," Mr Stewart told his son once the teacher left. "You want good grades, you're gonna have to earn them."

Life was back to normal . . . and it was so unfair. But at least there was gumbo for dinner.

Chapter Nine

It was getting to the point where Miley couldn't go anywhere without running into Jake Ryan. Days ago, she would have seen this as a good thing, a great thing even. Now, the morning after the Willis fiasco, Miley was anything but pleased. All she'd wanted was a peaceful day hanging out with Lilly and Oliver at Rico's. Maybe a little body-boarding. She didn't need to see Jake and be reminded of how embarrassed she should feel.

Sadly, the very sight of the guy made her want to bury her head in the sand. That she was at the beach where there was plenty of sand made her realize she could actually do this. Maybe burying her head would make her feel better. At least she wouldn't have to watch Jake and Holly cuddling for the cameras . . . *again.*

"You're gonna have to face him sooner or later," Lilly said solemnly.

Miley spotted Jake laughing with a bunch of guys. She figured they were probably laughing about her. "I choose later," she replied, turning on her heel to leave. But Lilly and Oliver were sick of the whole Jake-Miley thing and pulled her back. "All right, fine," she agreed. "But I can hear him already." She did her best Jake imitation: "'Hey, Miley. What are you and Willis doing tomorrow night? Hot date on the seesaw?'"

At the thought of Willis, Miley instantly turned glum. She'd wanted to strangle the kid at the bowling alley. But now, after a fitful night of sleep, she just felt bad for Willis. And terrible about herself: she'd been so mean! And to a kid! "I guess I do deserve this," she admitted. "I did use Willis."

Lilly was quick to agree. "Boy, did you ever!" she remarked. "It was like you had a love cold and he was the tissue. Willis, can I borrow you for a second?" Lilly pretended to blow her nose in a tissue, then tossed it away, calling out, "Goodbye, Willis."

Sometimes Lilly could be harsh. Then again, she was usually right. "I already admitted I was wrong!" Miley cried. "You don't have to blow my nose in it." She threw up her hands in frustration. "This is such a disaster!"

Oliver disagreed. "I bowled a two-eighty," he boasted. That was his highest bowling score yet, a score even some professionals would envy.

Lilly quickly reminded him that he'd been playing with Willis and Mike in the little kids' lane, meaning the bumpers blocking the gutter lanes were up.

"You never let me have anything!" Oliver complained.

A few of the guys who'd been talking to Jake walked over. "Hey, Miley," one called out, "we just heard –"

Miley braced herself for total and complete humiliation. "I know. I know," she interrupted him. "I went on a date with an eleven-year-old. But in my defence, he could totally pass for sixteen . . . without the balloon hat."

The guy looked at her like he had no idea what she was talking about. "I was just gonna tell you this funny joke Jake told us," he said, shaking his head in wonder. "But you going out with an eleven-year-old is so much funnier."

Always leave them laughing, thought Miley as the guys walked off, guffawing heartily at her expense. She sighed heavily.

"Maybe Jake didn't tell anybody," Lilly said.

"Why wouldn't he tell anybody? Any other boy would." Miley looked over at Jake. He was alone now. Could it be he'd really kept her secret a secret? And if so, why? He had to have a motive. What was it?

Her head overflowed with possible explanations. Maybe Jake was pretending to be nice because he'd already sent a mass e-mail to the class about her and her eleven-year-old "date." Maybe he'd even got a picture somehow and sent that out, too. Just her luck, Willis was probably wearing the balloon hat in the photo.

Then again, not everything had to be a conspiracy. Maybe Jake actually was a nice guy. After all, she saw a new side of him on the set of *Zombie High* when he'd confided his feelings about Miley to Hannah Montana.

"I've got to find out," she told Lilly, before stomping off to confront Jake.

Face-to-face with Jake, Miley got right down to business. "What's going on?" she demanded. "Why haven't you told anybody about me and balloon boy?"

Jake looked baffled. "Why would I

do that?" he asked her. "You seemed so miserable last night, I didn't want to make it any worse."

Well, this was too good to be true! What kind of stunt was this guy pulling? This had to be a game! He was acting! It had to be! Miley and Jake had spent the last few days taunting each other. And now Miley was supposed to believe he was being honest?

Except Jake sounded really sincere. She examined his face. She knew him well enough to know that if he'd been teasing her, he'd probably be smirking. Instead, he was smiling, looking entirely genuine.

And then, Miley made a fateful choice: she decided to believe Jake. Maybe because she wanted to, and maybe because it was the easiest thing to do. "That's . . . kinda nice," she told him.

Jake shrugged. "It's like I've been trying to tell you since the beginning; I'm really not a bad guy."

"Maybe not." Miley could feel herself softening.

"Plus, I thought it was kinda cool that you went to all that trouble just to make me jealous," he said.

Softening? Who said anything about softening? "Whoa, slow down there, ego boy," Miley told him. She was only willing to admit *so* much. "Why would I be trying to make you jealous? Besides, you have a girlfriend."

"Holly? She's not my girlfriend. We have a movie coming out so we've been hanging out as a publicity thing."

Miley couldn't believe it! All this time, he'd been shoving Holly in her face when they weren't even a real thing! "Why didn't you tell me that before?" she asked him.

"Well, I think I, uh –" Smooth Jake suddenly sounded flustered.

"Wait a minute!" Miley exclaimed before he could even say anything. "I know why. Because you were trying to make *me* jealous."

"Was not!" Jake blushed.

"Was, too!" Miley said triumphantly. "Admit it, Jake, you like me!"

Jake wasn't giving in so fast. "No, you like me! Just say it!"

"No, you say it!"

"No, you!"

Either Miley and Jake were both too stubborn, or they'd finally met their match. Whatever the case, they found themselves at a standoff. And, so, with nothing left to say, they did what they'd been wanting to do for so very long now.

They leaned towards each other – so close that Miley could feel a wisp of Jake's fringe tickle her forehead, so close that she could practically taste the thunder mint in his mouth – and kissed.

Chapter Ten

Sitting next to Jake, her hand clasped in his, Miley made a vow to herself: no more using people and no more games. It was such a waste of time. After all, had she been honest about her feelings for Jake at the Teen Scene Awards, she could have been feeling this great for days now.

"I guess this means we're kinda together," she remarked. The afternoon breeze blew through her hair.

"I guess it does," Jake said.

There were so many things in life that Miley had to pretend about. And while she wasn't ready to reveal herself as Hannah Montana to Jake, she wanted to be as up-front with him as possible. So while it crossed her mind that perhaps she should wait for him to ask her out, she quickly decided against it. Why wait when she could do it herself? "So, do you wanna go out sometime?" she asked, surprised at how she wasn't even nervous.

"Okay," Jake answered. "Would you like to go out four months from this Saturday?"

"Yeah," Miley replied, "that sounds —" Wait, four months from this Saturday? "Huh?"

"Frankie Muniz was gonna do this movie and he dropped out," Jake explained. "I fly to Romania tonight."

Miley had finally let her guard down, and now this?!? Jake was leaving! To be in a foreign country! Probably with some really gorgeous actress. Someone even hotter than Holly Shannon. "Yeah, but you can't just leave. You kissed me."

Jake blanched. "Hey, it's not my fault I got a big part in a movie."

"I know, but you kissed me!"

"I know, and it was great. And now I don't have to go off for four months and wonder what it would have been like."

Here Miley thought they'd just got together when really they were being wrenched apart! And Jake had known all along!

She'd been had!

Or had she . . . ?

Put your hands togeth-
er for the next Hannah
Montana book . . .

Face
the
Music

Adapted by Beth Beechwood

Based on the series created by Michael Poryes and Rich Correll & Barry O'Brien

Based on the episode, "Smells Like Teen Sellout," Written by Heather Wordham

Miley Stewart, dressed as Hannah Montana and made up to look extra glamorous, was standing on a set and practising her lines for a commercial she had agreed to do.

She looked deep into the camera. "My

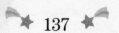

time is now . . ." she said in an overly dramatic whisper.

She held her hand in front of the camera, a bottle of perfume perched on her palm. "My perfume is Eau Wow," she breathed.

"Complete the circle." She pulled the top off the bottle. Right on cue, a group of acrobats wearing red unitards danced over and formed a human circle around her.

"I've never smelled anything like it before," Miley concluded with a smile.

After a brief pause, she dropped her "perfume character" voice and yelled, "Okay, where's that director, Hannah is ready to smell up the place?"

Lilly Truscott rushed over to her best friend. She was dressed as Lola, a member of Hannah's entourage, and was wearing an orange wig. "Let me smell, let me smell," she demanded, grabbing the bottle from Miley. She took a deep, appreciative sniff. "It's light, it's subtle. . . ."

"It's water," Miley offered.

"What a rip-off!" Lilly yelled in disgust.

"Lola, it's just a prop," Miley explained. "The real one will be here any second. It's been completely under wraps. Even I haven't smelled it."

"Then how do you know if it's any good?" Lilly asked suspiciously.

"Of course it's good," Miley said. "It's fifty bucks a bottle! And," she added meaningfully, "it completes the circle." Hearing their cue, the acrobats rolled by again.

"Who are those guys?" Lilly asked.

"I think they're the circle," Miley said. She practised her perfume pose, sucking in her cheeks like a model, just as Liza, the commercial's director, walked up.

"Ah, there's my gorgeous little star," she said. Miley turned around, thinking that Liza was referring to her. But the director blew right on by and walked over to where a perfume bottle was resting on a pillow. "I'm going to make you look fantastic. This is your moment," Liza said lovingly to the bottle as an armed security guard wheeled it onto the set.

"What am I, a plate of grits?" Miley complained.

"Here we go again," Liza said, turning her attention to Miley. She gave her a completely insincere smile. "Hannah, darling, I didn't see you there. When I found out we were going to work together again, all I could say was . . . yee-ha."

"Ah! Liza, you haven't changed a bit," Miley said emphatically.

"Fantastic," Liza grinned. "That means

the eye lift is working." She was nothing if not honest about her ongoing pursuit of perfection through plastic surgery.

At that moment, Miley's dad, Robby Stewart, also dressed in his usual "Hannah's entourage" disguise, walked up to the little group. Liza didn't see him, but he could certainly hear her.

"So where's that handsome cowboy daddy of yours?" she asked.

Miley saw her dad react in horror. He carefully started to back away from Liza, motioning to Miley that she should tell the director he wasn't there.

"He's in the bathroom," Miley said quickly.

"Oh," Liza said, her voice filled with hope. After all, if he was in the bathroom, eventually he'd have to come out – and that would be her moment to pounce!

Miley could see from her father's expression that this wasn't the message he wanted her to convey. She thought fast.

"In Europe," Miley lied.

"Oh," Liza said, this time with great disappointment.

"So, what do you say you give me that little bottle of liquid magic and we shoot ourselves a commercial?" Miley asked.